I0639213

Charles Follen Adams, Morgan J Sweeney

Dialect Ballads

Charles Follen Adams, Morgan J Sweeney

Dialect Ballads

ISBN/EAN: 9783742899606

Manufactured in Europe, USA, Canada, Australia, Japa

Cover: Foto ©Andreas Hilbeck / pixelio.de

Manufactured and distributed by brebook publishing software
(www.brebook.com)

Charles Follen Adams, Morgan J Sweeney

Dialect Ballads

DIALECT BALLADS

BY

CHARLES FOLLEN ADAMS

AUTHOR OF

"LEEDLE YAWCOB STRAUSS, AND OTHER POEMS"

ILLUSTRATED BY "BOZ"

NEW YORK

HARPER & BROTHERS, FRANKLIN SQUARE

1888

PREFACE.

In the preface of a previous volume ("Leedle Yawcob Strauss, and Other Poems") the plea is made that "the writer, moving only in the mercantile world, feels that he has wandered into forbidden ground, and craves the indulgence of the *literati* for these attempts to 'woo the Muse' during the few leisure hours allowed to members of his vocation." The kind reception accorded the above-named volume, both by the *literati* and the public at large, renders it entirely unnecessary for any further "craving" on the part of the author in presenting this volume of his subsequent work; not because he feels that it is free from faults and crudities, which are many, but because he hopes that the "one touch of nature that makes the whole world kin," even though expressed in homely, Anglo-Teutonic verse, will carry it, as it has its predecessor, to the great heart of the people, which he be-

7

lieves is still large enough to sympathize with the senior Strauss in his social troubles and daily perplexities.

Many of these poems have appeared in the columns of HARPER'S MAGAZINE, the *Detroit Free Press*, and other publications, and the present compilation is designed as a companion volume to "Leedle Yawcob Strauss, and Other Poems," with which it is nearly uniform in size and general style. The illustrations, like those in the previous volume, are from the pencil of Mr. M. J. Sweeney ("Boz"), for whose hearty co-operation the author is largely indebted.

CHARLES FOLLEN ADAMS.

CONTENTS.

CONTENTS.

MINE VAMILY.

DIMBLED scheeks, mit eyes off plue,
Mout' like id vas moisd mit dew,
Und leedle teeth shust peekin' droo—
    Dot's der baby.

11

Curly head, und full off glee,
Drowsers all oudt at der knee—
He vas peen blaying horse, you see—
    Dot's leedle Yawcob.

Von hundord·seexty in der shade,
Der oder day vhen she vas veighed—
She beats me soon, I vas avraid—
    Dot's mine Katrina.

Barefooted head, und pooty stoudt,
Mit grooked legs dot vill bend oudt,
Fond off his bier und sauer‑kraut—
Dot's me himself.

MINE VAMILY.

Von schmall young baby, full off fun,
Von leedle prite·eyed, roguish son,
Von frau to greet vhen vork vas done—
    Dot's mine vamily.

"AH-GOO!"

Vot vas id mine baby vas trying to say,
Vhen I goes to hees crib at der preak off der day?
Und oudt vrom der planket peeps ten leedle toes,
So pink und so shveet as der fresh plooming rose,
Und twisting und curling dhemselves all aboudt,
Shust like dhey vas saying, "Ve vant to get oudt!"
Vhile dot baby looks oup mit dhose bright eyes
    so plue,
Und don'd could say nodings, shust only,
      "Ah-goo!"

Vot vas id mine baby vas dinking aboudt,
Vhen dot thumb goes so qvick in hees shveet
    leedle mout',

Und he looks righdt avay, like he no undershtandt

Der reason he don'd could qvite shvallow hees
    handt;

Und he digs mit dhose fingers righdt into hees
    eyes,

Vhich fills hees oldt fader mit fear und surbrise;

Und vhen mit dhose shimnasdic dricks he vas
    droo,

He lay back und crow, und say nix budt
        " Ah - goo !"

Vot makes dot shmall baby shmile vhen he's
    ashleep;

Does he dink he vas blaying mit some von " bo-
    peep ?"

Der nurse say dhose shmiles vas der sign he haf
    colic—

More like dot he dhreams he vas hafing some
    frolic;

I feeds dot oldt nurse mit creen abbles some day
Und dhen eef *she* shmiles, I pelief vot she say;
Vhen dot baby got cramps he find someding to do
Oxcept shmile, und blay, und keep oup hees
"Ah - goo !"

I ask me, somedimes, vhen I looks in dot crib,
"Vill der shirdt-frondt, von day, dake der blace
off dot bib?
Vill dot plue-eyed baby dot's pooling mine hair
Know all vot I knows aboudt drouble und care?"
Dhen I dink off der vorldt, mit its bride und its
sins,
Und I vish dot mineself und dot baby vas tvins
Und all der day long I haf nodings to do
Budt shust laugh und crow, und keep saying,
"Ah - goo !"

"DON'D FEEL TOO BIG!"

A FROG vas a-singing von day in der brook
  (Id vas beddher, mine friends, you don'd feel
    too big!),

Und he shvelled mit pride, und he say, "Shust
    look;
Don'd I sing dhose peautiful songs like a book?"
    (Id vas beddher, mine friends, you don'd feel
    too big!)

A fish came a-shvimming along dot vay
    (Id vas beddher, mine friends, you don'd feel
        too big !);
' I'll dake you oudt off der vet," he say ;
Und der leedle froggie vas shtowed avay.
    (Id vas beddher, mine friends, you don'd feel
        too big !)

A hawk flew down und der fish dook in
  (Id vas beddher, mine friends, you don'd feel
    too big!);
Und der hawk he dink dot der shmardest vin
Vhen he shtuck his claws in dot fish's shkin.
  (Id vas beddher, mine friends, you don'd feel
    too big!)

24

A hunter vas oudt mit his gun aroundt
   (Id vas beddher, mine friends, you don'd feel
     too big!),
Und he say vhen der hawk vas brought to der
     groundt,
Und der fish und der leedle frog vas foundt,
   " It vas beddher, mine friends, you don'd feel
     too big!"

MINE MODER-IN-LAW.

DHERE vas many qveer dings, in dis land off der
    free,
  I neffer could qvite understand;
Der beoples dhey all seem so deefrent to me
  As dhose in mine own faderland.
Dhey gets blendy droubles, und indo mishaps,
  Mitoudt der least bit off a cause;
Und, vould you pelief id? dhose mean Yangee
    chaps,
  Dhey fights mit dheir moder-in-laws!

Shust dink off a vhite man so vicked as dot!
  Vhy not gife der oldt lady a show?

27

Who vas id gets oup, vhen der nighdt id vas
   hot,

Mit mine baby, I shust like to know?

Und dhen in der vinter, vhen Katrine vas sick,
  Und der mornings vas shnowy und raw,
Who made righdt avay oup dot fire so qvick?
  Vhy, dot vas mine moder-in-law.

Id vas von off dhose voman's righdts vellers, I
    been—
  Dhere vas nodings dot's mean aboudt me;
Vhen der oldt lady vishes to run dot masheen,
  Vhy, I shust lets her run id, you see.
Und vhen dot shly Yawcob vas cutting some
    dricks
  (A block off der oldt chip he vas, yaw!),
Eef she goes for dot chap like some dousands off
    bricks,
  Dot's all righdt! She's mine moder-in-law.

Veek oudt und veek in, id vas alvays der same,
  Dot romans vas boss off der house;

Budt, dhen, neffer mindt! I vas glad dot she
    came,
She vas kind to mine young Yawcob Strauss.

Und vhen dhere vas vater to get vrom der
  shpring,
Und fire-vood to shplit oup und saw,
She vas velcome to do id. Dhere's not anyding
  Dot's too goot for mine moder-in-law.

YAW, DOT ISH SO!

Yaw, dot ish so! Yaw, dot ish so!
"Dis vorldt vas all a fleeting show."
  I shmokes mine pipe,
  I trinks mine bier,
Und efry day to vork I go;
"Dis vorldt vas all a fleeting show;"
  Yaw, dot ish so!

Yaw, dot ish so! Yaw, dot ish so!
I don'd got mooch down here below,
  I eadt und trink,
  I vork und shleep,

Und find oudt, as I oldter grow,
I haf a hardter row to hoe;
  Yaw, dot ish so!

Yaw, dot ish so! Yaw, dot ish so!
Dis vorldt don'd gife me haf a show;
  Somedings to vear,
  Some food to eadt;
Vot else? Shust vait a minude, dough;
Katrina, und der poys! Oho!
  Yaw, dot ish so!

Yaw, dot ish so! Yaw, dot ish so!
Dis vorldt don'd been a fleeting show.
  I haf mine frau,
  I haf mine poys,
To cheer me daily, as I go;
Dot's pest as anydings I know;
  Yaw, dot ish so!

34

DER SHPIDER UND DER FLY.

I READS in Yawcob's shtory book,
  A couple veeks ago,
Von firsd-rade boem, vot I dinks
  Der beoples all should know.

Id ask dis goot conundhrum, too,
   Vich ve should brofit by:
" 'Vill you indo mine barlor valk?'
   Says der shpider off der fly."

Dot set me dinking, righdt avay,
   Und vhen, von afdernoon,
A shbeculator he cooms in,
   Und dells me, pooty soon,

He haf a silfer mine to sell,
 Und ask me eef I puy,
I dink off der oxberience
 Off dot plue·pottle fly.

Der oder day, vhen on der cars
 I vent py Nie Yorck, oudt,
I meets a fräulein on der train,
 Who dold me, mit a pout,

DER SHPIDER UND DER FLY.

She likes der Deutscher shentlemens,
    Und dells me sit peside her—
I dinks, maype, I vas der fly,
    Und she vas peen der shpider.

I vent indo der shmoking · car,
    Vhere dhey vas blaying boker,
Und also haf somedings dhey calls
    Der funny "leedle joker."

Some money id vas shanging hands,
  Dhey wanted me to try—
I says, "You vas too brevious;
  I don'd vas peen a fly!"

On Central Park a shmardt young man
  Says, "Strauss, how vas you peen?"
Und dake me kindly py der hand,
  Und ask off mine Katrine.

39

He vants to shange a feefty bill,
　　Und says hees name vas Schneider—
Maype, berhaps he vas all righdt;
　　More like he vas a shpider.

Mosd efry day some shvindling chap,
　　He dries hees leedle game;
I cuts me oudt dot shpider biece,
　　Und poot id in a frame;
Righdt in mine shtore I hangs id oup,
　　Und near id, on der shly,
I geeps a glub, to send gvick oudt
　　Dhose shpiders "on der fly."

MINE SCHILDHOOD.

Der schiltren dhey vas poot in ped,
  All tucked oup for der nighdt;
I dakes mine pipe der mantel off,
  Und py der fireside prighdt
I dinks aboudt vhen I vas young—
  Off moder, who vas tead,
Und how at nighdt—like I do Hans—
  She tucked me oup in ped.

I mindt me off mine fader, too,
  Und how he yoost to say,
"Poor poy, you haf a hardt oldt row
  To hoe, und leedle blay!"

I find me oudt dot id vas drue
  Vot mine oldt fader said,
Vhile smoodhing down mine flaxen hair
  Und tucking me in ped.

Der oldt folks! Id vas like a dhream
  To shpeak off dhem like dot.
Gretchen und I vas "oldt folks" now,
  Und haf two schiltren got.
Ve lofes dhem more as neffer vas,
  Each leedle curly head,
Und efry nighdt ve takes dhem oup
  Und tucks dhem in dheir ped.

Budt dhen, somedimes, vhen I feels plue,
  Und all dings lonesome seem,
I vish I vas dot poy again,
  Und dis vas all a dhream.

I vant to kiss mine moder vonce,
　Und vhen mine brayer vas said,
To haf mine fader dake me oup
　Und tuck me in mine ped.

DER VATER-MILL.

I READS aboudt dot vater-mill dot runs der life-
long day,

Und how der vater don'd coom pack vhen vonce
id flows avay;

Und off der mill-shtream dot glides on so beace-
fully und shtill,

Budt don'd vas putting in more vork on dot same
vater-mill.

Der boet says 'tvas beddher dot you holdt dis
broverb fast—

" Der mill id don'd vould grind some more mit
vater dot vas past."

Dot boem id vas peautiful to read aboudt; dot's
    so !

Budt eef dot vater *vasn't* past how could dot mill-
    vheel go ?

Und vhy make drouble mit dot mill vhen id vas
    been inclined

To dake each obbordunidy dot's gifen id to
    grind ?

Und vhen der vater cooms along in qvandidies
    so vast,

Id lets some oder mill dake oup der vater dot
    vas past.

Dhen der boet shange der subject, und he dells
    us vonce again,

"Der sickle neffer more shall reap der yellow,
    garnered grain."

Vell, vonce vas blendy, aind't id ? Id vouldn't
    been so nice

To haf dot sickle reaping oup der same grain
ofer tvice!

Vhy, vot's der use off cutting oup der grass al-
reaty mown?

Id vas pest, mine moder dold me, to let vell
enough alone.

"Der summer vinds refife no more leaves strewn
o'er earth und main."

Vell, who vants to refife dhem? Dhere vas blendy more again!

Der summer vinds dhey shtep righdt oup iu goot
time to brepare

Dhose blants und trees for oder leaves; dhere soon
vas creen vous dhere.

Shust bear dis adverb on your mindts, mine
frendts, und holdt id fast:

Der new leaves don'd vas been aroundt undil der
oldt vas past.

Dhen neffer mindt der leaves dot's dead; der
grain dot's in der bin;

Dhey both off dhem haf had dheir day, und shust
vas gathered in.

Und neffer mindt der vater vhen id vonce goes
droo der mill;

Ids vork vas done! Dhere's blendy more dot
vaits ids blace to fill.

Let each von dake dis moral, vrom der king down
to der peasant—

Don'd mindt der vater dot vas past, budt der
vater dot vas bresent.

DER OAK UND DER VINE.

I DON'D vas preaching voman's righdts,
  Or anyding like dot,
Und I likes to see all beoples
  Shust gondented mit dheir lot;
Budt I vants to gondradict dot shap
  Dot made dis leedle shoke:

"A voman vas der glinging vine,
  Und man der shturdy oak."

Berhaps, somedimes, dot may be drue,
  Budt, den dimes oudt off nine,
I find me oudt dot man himself
  Vas been der glinging vine;

51

Und vhen hees friendts dhey all vas gone,
  Und he vas shust "tead proke,"
Dot's vhen der voman shteps righdt in,
  Und been der shturdy oak.

Shust go oup to der paseball groundts
  Und see dhose "shturdy oaks"

All planted roundt ubon der seats—
  Shust hear dheir laughs und shokes!
Dhen see dhose vomens at der tubs,
  Mit glothes oudt on der lines:
Vhich vas der shturdy oaks, mine frendts,
  Und vhich der glinging vines?

Vhen Sickness in der householdt comes,
  Und veeks und veeks he shtays,

Who vas id fighdts him mitoudt resdt,
  Dhose veary nighdts und days?
Who beace und gomfort alvays prings,
  Und cools dot fefered prow?
More like id vas der tender vine
  Dot oak he glings to now.

"Man vants budt leedle here pelow,"
  Der boet von time said;

Dhere's leedle dot man he *don'd* vant,
   I dink id means, inshted;
Und vhen der years keep rolling on,
   Dheir cares und droubles pringing,
He vants to pe der shturdy oak,
   Und, also, do der glinging.

Maype, vhen oaks dhey gling some more,
   Und don'd so shturdy been,
Der glinging vines dhey haf some shance
   To helb run Life's masheen.
In helt und sickness, shoy und pain,
   In calm or shtormy veddher,
'Tvas beddher dot dhose oaks und vines
   Should alvays gling togeddher.

MINE SHILDREN.

On, dhose shildren, dhose shildren, dhey boddher
    mine life!
Vhy don'd dhey keep qviet, like Katrine, mine
    vife?
Vot makes dhem so shock fool off mischief, I vun
    der,
A-shumping der room roundt mit noises like duu
    der?
Hear dot! Vas dhere anyding make sooch a noise
As Yawcob und Otto, mine two leedle poys?

Ven I dake oup mine pipe for a goot qviet shmoke
Dhey crawl me all ofer, und dink id a shoke

To go droo mine bockets to see vot dhey find,
Und if mit der latch-key mine vatch dhey can vind.
I'd dakes someding more as dheir fader und moder
To qviet dot Otto und his leedle broder.

Dhey shtub oudt dheir boots, und vear holes in
    der knees
Off dheir drousers und shtockings, und sooch
    dings as dhese.
I dink if dot Crœsus vas lifing to-day,
Dhose poys make more bills as dot Kaiser could
    pay;
I find me qvick oudt dot some riches dake vings,
Ven each gouple a tays I must buy dhem new
    dings.

I pring dhose two shafers some toys efry tay.
Pecause "Shonny Schwartz has sooch nice dings,"
    dhey say,

"Und Shonny Schwartz' barents vas poorer as
 ve "—
Dot's vot der young rashkells vas saying to me.
Dot oldt Santa Klaus, mit a shleigh fool off toys,
Don'd gif sadisfactions to dhose greedy poys.

Dhey kick der clothes off vhen ashleep in dheir
 ped,
Und get so mooch croup dot dhey almosdt vas
 dead;
Budt id don'd made no tifferent: before id vas light
Dhey vas oup in der morning mit pillows to fight;
I dink id was beddher you don'd got some ears
Vhen dhey blay "Holdt der Fort," und dhen gif
 dree cheers.

Oh, dhose shildren, dhose shildren, dhey boddher
 mine life!—
But shtop shust a leedle. If Katrine, mine vife,

Und dhose leedle shildren, dhey don'd been
    around,
Und all droo der house dhere vas neffer a sound—
Vell, poys, vhy you look oup dot vay mit surbrise?
I guess dhey see tears in dheir old fader's eyes.

DER DEUTSCHER'S MAXIM.

DHERE vas vot you call a maxim
  Dot I hear der oder day,
Und I wride id in mine album,
  So id don'd could got avay;
Und I dells mine leedle Yawcob
  He moost mind vot he's aboudt:

" 'Tis too late to lock der shtable
   Vhen der horse he vas gone oudt."

Vhen I see ubon der corners
   Off der shtreets, most efry night,
Der loafers und der hoodlums,
   Who do nix but shvear und fight,
I says to mine Katrina,
   "Let us make home bright und gay;

Ve had petter lock der shtable,
So our colts don'd got avay."

Vhen you see dhose leedle urchins,
Not mooch ofer knee-high tall,
Shump righdt indo der melon-patch,
Shust owf der garden vall,

Und vatch each leedle rashkell
Vhen he cooms back mit hees "boodle,"

64

Look oudt und lock your shtable,
   So your own nag don'd shkydoodle!

Vhen der young man at der counter
   Vants to shpecgulate in shtocks,
Und buys hees girl some timond rings,
   Und piles righdt 'oup der rocks,

E   65

Look oudt for dot young feller;
  Id vas safe enuff to say
Dot der shtable id vas empty,
  Und der horse vas gone avay.

Dhen dake Time by der fetlock:
  Don'd hurry droo life's courses;
Rememper vot der boet says,
  "Life's but a shpan"—off horses.
Der poy he vas der comin' man;
  Be careful vhile you may;
Shust keep der shtable bolted,
  Und der horse don'd got avay.

"CUT, CUT BEHIND!"

Vhen shnow und ice vas on der ground,
  Und merry shleigh-bells shingle;
Vhen Shack Frost he vas been around,
  Und makes mine oldt ears tingle—
I hear dhose roguish *gamins* say,
  "Let shoy pe unconfined!"
Und dhen dhey go for efry shleigh,
  Und yell, "Cut, cut pehind!"

It makes me shust feel young some more
  To hear dhose youngsters yell,
Und eef I don'd vas shtiff und sore,
  Py shings! I shust vould—vell,

Vhen some oldt pung vas coomin' py,
    I dink I'd feel inclined
To shump righdt in upon der shly,
    Und shout, "Cut, cut pehind!"

I mind me vot mine fader said
    Vonce, vhen I vas a poy,
Mit meeschief alvays in mine head,
    Und fool off life und shoy.
"Now, Hans, keep off der shleighs," says he,
    "Or else shust bear in mind,
I dake you righdt across mine knee,
    Und cut, cut, cut pehind!"

Vell, dot vas years und years ago,
    Und mine young Yawcob, too,
Vas now shkydoodling droo der shnow,
    Shust like I used to do;

"CUT, CUT BEHIND!"

Und vhen der pungs coom py mine house,
    I shust peeks droo der plind,
Und sings oudt, "Go id, Yawcob Strauss,
    Cut, cut, cut, cut pehind!"

A ZOOLOGICAL ROMANCE.

Inspired by an Unusual Flow of Animal Spirits.

No sweeter girl ewe ever gnu
Than Betty Marten's daughter Sue.

With sable hare, small tapir waist,
And lips you'd gopher miles to taste;

Bright, lambent eyes, like the gazelle,
Sheep pertly brought to bear so well;

Ape pretty lass, it was avowed,
Of whom her marmot to be proud.

72

Deer girl! I loved her as my life,
And vowed to heifer for my wife.

Alas! a sailor, on the sly,
Had cast on her his wether eye –

He said my love for her was bosh,
And my affection I musquash.

He'd dog her footsteps everywhere,
Anteater in the easy-chair.

He'd setter round, this sailor chap,
And pointer out upon the map

The spot where once a cruiser boar
Him captive to a foreign shore.

The cruel captain far outdid
The yaks and crimes of Robert Kid.

He oft would whale Jack with the cat,
And say, "My buck, doe you like that?

"What makes you stag around so, say!
The catamounts to something, hey?"

Then he would seal it with an oath,
And say, "You are a lazy sloth!

"I'll starve you down, my sailor fine,
Until for beef and porcupine!"

And, fairly horse with fiendish laughter,
Would say, "Henceforth, mind what giraffe ter!"

In short, the many risks he ran
Might well a llama braver man.

Then he was wrecked and castor shore
While feebly clinging to anoa;

Hyena cleft among the rocks
He crept, *sans* shoes and minus ox;

And when he fain would goat to bed,
He had to lion leaves instead.

Then Sue would say, with troubled face,
"How koodoo live in such a place?"

And straightway into tears would melt,
And say, "How badger must have felt!"

While he, the brute, woodchuck her chin,
And say, " Aye-aye, my lass!" and grin.

* * * * * * *

Excuse these steers. . . . It's over now;
There's naught like grief the hart can cow.

Jackass'd her to be his, and she—
She gave Jackal and jilted me.

And now, alas! the little minks
Is bound to him with Hymen's lynx.

THE YOUNG TRAMP.

HELLO, thar, stranger! Whar yer frum?
Come in and make yerself ter hum!
We're common folks—ain't much on style;
Come in and stop a little while;
'Twon't do no harm ter rest yer some.

Youngster, yer pale, and don't look well!
What, way frum Bosting? Naow, dew tell!
Why, that's a hundred mile or so;
What started yer, I'd like ter know,
On sich a tramp; got goods ter sell?

No home—no friends? Naow that's too bad!
Wall, cheer up, boy, and don't be sad—

Wife, see what yer can find ter eat,
And put the coffee on ter heat—
We'll fix yer up all right, my lad.

Willing ter work, can't git a job,
And not a penny in yer fob?
Wall, naow, that's rough, I dew declare!
What, tears? Come, youngster, I can't bear
Ter see yer take on so, and sob.

How came yer so bad off, my son?
Father was killed? 'Sho'; whar? Bull Run?
Why, I was in that scrimmage, lad,
And got used up, too, pretty bad;
I sha'n't forgit old 'sixty - one!

So yer were left in Bosting, hey?
A baby when he went away—

Those Bosting boys were plucky, wife,
Yer know one of 'em saved my life,
Else I would not be here to · day.

'Twas when the " Black Horse Cavalcade "
Swept down upon our small brigade
I got the shot that made me lame,
When down on me a trooper came,
And this 'ere chap struck up his blade.

Poor feller! He was stricken dead;
The trooper's sabre cleaved his head.
Joe Billings was my comrade's name ;
He was a Bosting boy, and game!
I almost wished I'd died instead.

Why, lad ! what makes yer tremble so ?
Your father ! what, my comrade Joe ?

F

And you his son? Come ter my heart!
My home is yours; I'll try, in part,
Ter pay his boy the debt I owe.

MOTHER'S DOUGHNUTS.

El Dorado, 1851.

I'VE jest bin down ter Thompson's, boys,
  'N' feelin' kind o' blue,
I thought I'd look in at "The Ranch,"
  Ter find out what wuz new,
When I seen this sign a-hangin'
  On a shanty by the lake:
"Here's whar yer gets yer doughnuts
  Like yer mother used ter make."

I've seen a grizzly show his teeth;
  I've seen Kentucky Pete
Draw out his shooter 'n' advise
  A "tenderfoot" ter treat;

But nuthin' ever tuk me down,
　'N' made my benders shake,
Like that sign about the doughnuts
　Like my mother used ter make.

A sort o' mist shut out the ranch,
　'N' standin' thar instead
I seen an old white farm-house,
　With its doors all painted red.
A whiff came through the open door—
　Wuz I sleepin' or awake?
The smell wuz that of doughnuts
　Like my mother used ter make.

The bees wuz hummin' round the porch
　Whar honeysuckles grew;
A yellow dish of apple sass
　Wuz sittin' thar in view;

85

'N' on the table by the stove
  An old-time "johnny-cake,"
'N' a platter full of doughnuts
  Like my mother used ter make.

A patient form I seemed ter see,
  In tidy dress of black;
I almost thought I heard the words,
  "When will my boy come back?"
'N' then—the old sign creaked;
  But now it wuz the boss who spake,
"Here's whar yer gets yer doughnuts
  Like yer mother used ter make."

Well, boys, that kind o' broke me up,
  'N' ez I've "struck pay gravel,"
I ruther think I'll pack my kit,
  Vamose the ranch, 'n' travel.

I'll make the old folks jubilant,
    'N', ef I don't mistake,
I'll try some o' them doughnuts
    Like my mother used ter make.

HE DIDN'T UNDERSTAND.

"PRAY how is your daughter, friend Scroggins?
    I hear that she had quite a fall
While dancing the German, last evening,
    At Montague's *recherche* ball.

"I'm sorry Miss Laura was injured,
    And hope that no serious harm
Will ensue from the fall; I assure you
    Wife and I were quite filled with alarm.

"Those dresses with trails are a nuisance;
    They didn't wear them in *our* day.
No wonder that accidents happen
    With such things to get in one's way.

89

"When *we* used to dance, my dear Scroggins,
   There were no such 'pullbacks' as these
To mar our delight in the 'mazy,'
   And trip us, perchance, on our knees.

"You could balance, and go down the centre,
   And dance the Virginia reel,
Without walking half up a panier,
   With the bustle caught on to your heel.

"Mrs. Grundy called over this morning,
   And said, with a smirk and grimace,
That Laura, last night at the party,
   Was horribly banged round the face.

"So I thought I'd come over and ask you
   If she was improving to-day,
And if we could be of assistance
   In any conceivable way.

" Mrs. Grundy said—"   "Zounds, Mr. Jenkins,
Just tell Mrs. G. to be hanged!
There's nothing the matter with Laura;
'Twas her hair, not her face, that was ' banged.' "

ROLLER-SKATING.

IN FOUR ACTS.

ACT I.

"Ho, ho!" said careless Willie Gates;
"Who couldn't learn on roller-skates?"

ACT II.

" Ah, ha !" said he, as on the floor
He struck out boldly for the door.

ACT III.

" So, so !" observed the roller·skates,
" We'll interview young William Gates."

93

ACT IV.

"Oh! Oo-o-o!" said Willie, meek and humble,
"I thought 'twas easy; *now I 'tumble.*'"

PREVALENT POETRY.

A WANDERING tribe, called the Siouxs,
Wear moccasins, having no shiouxs;
    They are made of buckskin,
    With the fleshy side in,
Embroidered with beads of bright hyiouxs.

When out on the war-path, the Siouxs
March single file — never by tiouxs—
    And by "blazing" the trees
    Can return at their ease,
And their way through the forests ne'er liouxs.

All new-fashioned boats he eschiouxs,
And uses the birch-bark caniouxs;

These are handy and light,
And, inverted at night,
Give shelter from storms and from diouxs.

The principal food of the Siouxs
Is Indian maize, which they briouxs,
    And hominy make,
    Or mix in a cake,
And eat it with pork, as they chiouxs.

*   *   *   *   *   *   *

Now, doesn't this spelling look cyiouxrious?
'Tis enough to make any one fyiouxrious!
    So a word to the wise!—
    Pray our language revise
With orthography not so injiouxrious.

THANKSGIVING.

Within a garret, cold and forlorn,
A group is gathered Thanksgiving morn:

Father and mother, with children three—
One but a babe on the mother's knee.

Haggard and pale is the father's face,
Where lingering sickness has left its trace:

While the careworn look on the mother's brow
Tells of the sorrow upon her now.

G 97

Hungry and faint from the lack of food,
With scanty clothing, no coal nor wood;

A broken table, a bare pine floor—
What have they to be thankful for?

Thoughts like these to the parents come,
While sitting here in their cheerless home.

The children, nestled upon the bed,
A fragment of carpet over them spread,

Are blind to their parents' mute despair;
And the little girl, with a pitying air,

Says, " What do *poor* children do, I wonder,
With no warm carpet to cuddle under;

"No papa and mamma to give 'em bread,
And tuck 'em up when they go to bed?"

Tear-drops start from the father's eyes;
Prayers from the mother's lips arise.

*   *   *   *   *   *   *

Footsteps fall on the creaking floor;
A knock is heard on the chamber door.

A bluff "Good-morning" their query brings,
And, "Sambo, you rascal, fetch up the things!"

While the squire's darkey, with cheerful grin,
Food and clothing brings quickly in.

"Lord bless you, ma'am! why, who'd a knowed
That folks lived up in this 'ere abode?

"'Tain't fit for a barn, 'n', ez I'm a sinner,
I'll take you all to my house to dinner.

"I'll find you work when you're strong and well,
'N' a better place than this 'ere to dwell—"

And the squire paused, while a tear arose,
And dropped unseen on his ruby nose,

As the baby boy, with a happy look,
A rosy apple from Sambo took,

And the children gathered, with hungry eyes,
'Round the platter of doughnuts and pumpkin
    pies;

While the grateful mother could only say,
"Truly, this *is* Thanksgiving Day!"

THE BUTCHER'S COURTSHIP.

"Oh, my Mary Ann," he side,
"Will you be my loving bride?
I cannot liver 'nother day without you.
  Your bright smile lights up my heart,
  Whisper yes, beefore we part,
And the tenderlines of love I'll cast about you!"

Then the rascal, growing bolder,
Drew her head upon his shoulder,
While the ribbones on her bonnet fluttered free,
  And fore-quarter of an hour
  They reclined within the bower,
And she promised him she ever true would be.

"Now," says he, "I must be goin'—
Don't you hear the cattle loin?
I can tarry here no longer, love, to-day;
    You can steak a silver dollar
    I shall be a steady caller;
Keep your pluck and spirits up while I'm away!"

    Then he turned to cross a mead
    Where the horned cattle feed,
And wasn't paying very much attention
    To the gender of the herd,
    When there suddenly occurred
An accident he fain would never mention.

    He chanced to look a round,
    When towards him, with a bound,
Came their masculine protector o'er the lea:

And so brisket seemed to him
That his chance was rather slim
To flank him, or to even shin a tree.

He was bull dosed, so to speak,
Sorely rumpled, cowed and weak,
And will steer hereafter clear from bulls and cows.
The tail, alas! is sad;
Would'st shun a bull that's mad?
Then beware the quick contraction of his browse!

MY INFUNDIBULIFORM HAT.

The scenes of my childhood, how oft I recall!
The sports of my youth, with my kite, top, and
    ball;
And that happy day when, with spirits elate,
I took my first step towards manhood's estate,
With a new coat and vest, bosom shirt and cra-
    vat,
And *début* with my infundibuliform hat.

How I stooped beneath awnings full seven feet
    high,
To the no small delight of my friends passing
    by;

And the sport that I made for the boys at the
    store
When I "chalked" at the height of my "tile"
    on the door;
One foot and two inches—I think it was that—
My guess on that infundibuliform hat.

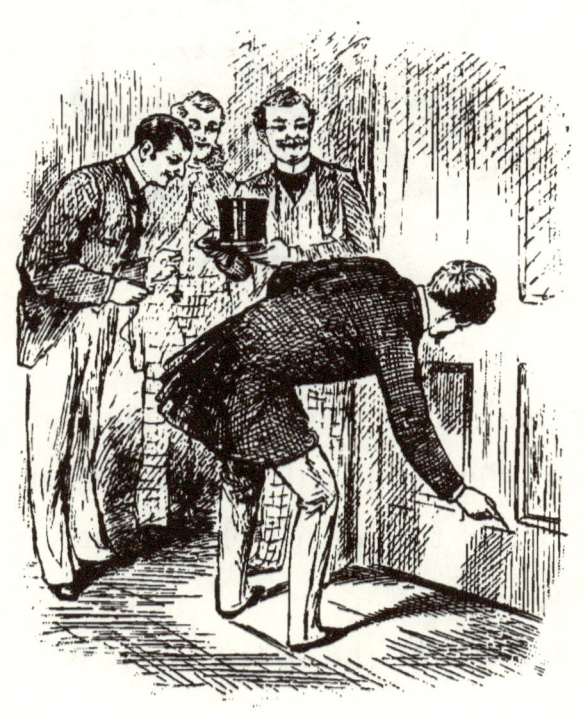

Then my maiden attempt as a maiden's gallant
When I proffered my elbow, with glances aslant;
And the walk to her dwelling that evening so
    fair,
Not to speak of the *téte·à·téte* when we got
    there,

The forfeit I claimed, as together we sat,
When she tried on my infundibuliform hat.

* * * * * * *

Well! boys will be boys, and we men, after all,
Would gladly be freed from Time's pitiless thrall,
And live those days over, when, single and free—
Zounds! wife's looking over my shoulder to see
What I have been writing. . . . Well, we've had
   a spat,
And she smashed my infundibuliform hat.

THE LITTLE CONQUEROR.

" ' 'Twas midnight; not a sound was heard
   Within the ' "—" Papa ! won't 'ou 'ook
An' see my pooty 'ittle house ?
   I wis' 'ou wouldn't wead 'ou book "—

" ' Within the palace, where the king
   Upon his couch in anguish lay ' "—
" Papa !   Pa-*pa !* I wis' 'ou'd tum
   An' have a 'ittle tonty play "—

" ' No gentle hand was there to bring
   The cooling draught, or bathe his brow;
His courtiers and his pages gone ' "—
   " Tum, papa, tum; I want 'ou *now* "—

112

Down goes the book with needless force,
  And, with expression far from mild,
With sullen air and clouded brow,
  I seat myself beside the child.

Her little trusting eyes of blue
  With mute surprise gaze in my face,
As if in its expression stern
  Reproof and censure she could trace.

Anon her little bosom heaves,
  Her rosy lips begin to curl;
And with a quiv'ring chin she sobs,
  "Papa don't 'uv' his 'ittle dirl!"

King, palace, book—all are forgot;
  My arms are 'round my darling thrown—
The thunder-cloud has burst, and lo!
  Tears fall and mingle with her own.

DOT LEEDLE LOWEEZA.

How dear to dis heart vas mine grandshild Low-
    eeza !
  Dot shveet leedle taughter off Yawcob, mine son !
I nefer vas tired to hug und to shqveeze her
    Vhen home I gets back, und der day's vork
    vas done.

Vhen I vas avay, oh, I know dot she miss me,
   For vhen I come homevards she rushes bell-
      mell,
Und poots oup dot shveet leedle mout' for to kiss
      me—
   Her "darling oldt gampa," dot she lofe so vell.

Katrina, mine frau, she could not do mitoudt her,
   She vas sooch a gomfort to her, day py day:

Dot shild she make efry von habby aboudt her,
  Like sunshine she drife all dheir troubles avay.
She holdt der vool yarn vhile Katrina she vind it,
  She pring her dot camfire bottle to shmell;
She fetch me mine pipe, too, vhen I don'd can find it,
  Dot plue-eyed Loweeza, dot lofe me so vell.

How shveet, vhen der toils off der veek vas all ofer,
  Und Sunday vas come, mit its qviet und rest,

To valk mit dot shild 'mong der daisies und
    clofer,
  Und look off der leedle birds building dheir
    nest!
Her pright leedle eyes, how dhey shparkle mit
    pleasure!
  Her laugh it rings oudt shust so clear like a
    bell;
I dink dhere vas nopody haf sooch a treas-
    ure
As dot shmall Loweeza, dot lofe me so vell.

Vhen vinter vas come, mit its coldt, shtormy
    veddher,
  Katrina und I ve musd sit in der house,
Und dalk off der bast by der fireside toged-
    dher,
  Or blay mit dot taughter off our Yawcob
    Strauss.

Oldt age, mit its wrinkles, pegins to remind us
    Ve gannot shtay long mit our shildren to
        dvell;
But soon ve shall meet mit der poys left pehind
        us,
    Und dot shveet Loweeza, dot lofe us so vell.

MINE KATRINE.

You vouldn't dink mine *frau*,
If you shust look at her now,
Vhere der wrinkles on her prow
    Long haf been,
Vas der *fräulein* blump und fair,
Mit der wafy flaxen hair,
Who did vonce mine heart enshuare—
    Mine Katrine.

Der dime seems shord to me
Since ve game acrosd der sea,
To der gountry off der free
    Ve'd neffer seen;

Bud ve hear der beople say
Dhere vas vork und blendy bay,
So I shtarted righdt avay
　　　Mit Katrine.

Oh, der shoy dot filled mine house
Vhen dot goot oldt Toctor Krauss
Brought us "Leedle Yawcob Strauss,"
　　　Shveet und clean;
Vhy, I don'd pelief mine eyes
Vhen I look, now, mit surbrise,
On dot feller, shust der size
　　　Off Katrine!

Den "dot leedle babe off mine,"
He vas grown so tall und fine—
Shust so sdrait as any pine
　　　You effer seen,

Und der beoples all agree
Sooch fine poys dhey neffer see.
(Dhey looks much more like me
    As Katrine.)

Vell, ve haf our criefs und shoys,
Und dhere's naught our lofe destroys,
Budt I miss dhose leedle poys
    Dot used to been;
Und der tears vill somedime sdart,
Und I feels so sick at heart,
Vhen I dinks I soon must part
    From Katrine.

Oldt Time vill soon pe here,
Mit his sickle und his shpear,
Und vill vhisper in mine ear
    Mit sober mien:

"You must coom along mit me,
For id vas der Lord's decree;
Und von day dhose poys you'll see
Und Katrine."

VERSIFIED PUNS.

Some running rhymes, neither profound nor wise,
To swell this book to a convenient size.

CRYPTOGAMIC.

Augustus and Nelly were walking
    Through the meadow, one bright summer day,
And merrily laughing and talking,
    When some toadstools they saw by the way.
" Do the toads really use these to sit on ?"
    Said Nelly—" now don't make a pun, Gus,
If you do, like the subject we've hit on,
    I'll deem it the meanest of fun - Gus."

PENNY WISE.

" Can you tell me," said a punster
　Who had in our sanctum popped,
And upon the floor was seeking
　For a penny he had dropped—

" Can you tell me why, at present,
　I am like Noah's weary dove?"
And he glanced with inward tremor
　Towards a gun that hung above.

" Would'st thou know?" he queried, blandly,
　As he dodged the cudgel stout
Which we shied at him in anger—
　" 'Tis because I'm one cent out."

ADVICE FOR THE NEW YEAR.

Schpend someding less as vot you earns;
　Pay all der notes vhen dhey comes due;
Don'd you forget von half you learns,
　Nor bite off dwice vot you can chew.

A FLOORER.

Says Pat to his girl, " Be the Powers,
　A conondhrum I hev fur ye, dear !
Why are ye like the goddess of flowers?
　Sure ye nivir will guess it, I fear !

"The ansor I'll be afther givin':
　Now thin, d'ye mind, me swate Nora ?
It's two shtories high ye are livin',
　That makes ye a rale second Flora !"

GOING THROUGH THE RYE.

Says the Captain to Pat,
　" Come, I'll have none o' that !"
As Paddy of whiskey was drinking his fill.
　With a satisfied sigh,
　As he finished the " rye,"
Says Paddy, " Be Jabers, I don't think ye will !"

127

ALL IN HIS EYE.

He jumped on board the railway train,
And cried, "Farewell! Lucinda Jane,
    My precious, sweet Lucinda!"
Alas! how soon he changed his cry,
And, while the tear stood in his eye,
    He said, "Confound Loose Cinder!"

FALL POETRY.

A certain young woman, named Hannah,
Slipped down on a piece of banana;
        She shrieked, and oh - my'd!
        And more stars she spied
Than belongs to the star - spangled banner.

A gentleman sprang to assist her,
And picked up her muff and her wrister.
        "Did you fall, ma'am?" he cried;
        "Do you think," she replied,
"I sat down for the fun of it, Mister?"

128

EARLY RISING.

"... Rise with the lark,
And with the lark to bed—"

Why for a pattern choose the lark—
Rise in the morn while yet 'tis dark,
And with the early bird to bed repair?
Why not take bruin for example?
Of promptness, pray, what better sample?
'Tis said there's nothing s'urly as a bear.

TIME'S CHANGES.

'Twas in Arabia's sunny land
He wooed his bonny bride;
His umber Ella, rain or shine,
Was ever by his side;
But now he does not Kaffir her,
No love tale does he tell her;
He'd fain Bedouin something else—
Alas! poor Arab - Ella.

I   129

HOME MEMORIES.

"Be it ever so humble,
There's no place like home!"

I'm sitting again 'neath the old elm - tree's shade,
And viewing the fields where in childhood I
strayed;
The breeze fans my cheek, and the birds go and
come,
While I listen, entranced, to the bee's soothing hum.

Hum, hum—sweet, sweet hum!
Tho' it ever so humble - bee—
—!!—!!!*** He's stung me I vum!

COUNTRY SOUNDS.

The humming of the bees,
Wafted on the scented breeze,
And the robin's tender notes are very fine;
But sweeter, far, to me
Than the humming of the bee
Is the melting tender loin' of the kine.

130

THE BACHELOR'S CONSOLATION.

Oh, dear! this gout and rheumatiz,
    I fear I shall go wild!
But though I am a bachelor,
    And have no chick nor child,
I know that when I am no more—
    Let folks say what they please—
Although I have no kith nor kin,
    I'll have my leg - at - ees.

PAT'S LOGIC.

"The greatest burd to foight," says Pat,
    " Barring the agle, is the duck;
He has a foine large bill to peck,
    And plinty of rale Irish pluck.

"And, thin, d'ye moind the fut he has?
    Full as broad over as a cup;
Show me the fowl upon two ligs
    That's able fer to thrip him up!"

THE LOVER'S LAMENT.

"'Im sitting on this tile, Mary,"
   He said, in accents sad,
Removing from the rocking - chair
   The best silk hat he had;
And while he viewed the shapeless mass,
   That erst was trim and neat,
He murmured, "Would it had been felt
   Before I took my seat!"

ALMOST AN ARGONAUT.

'Twus in the fall of 'forty - nine
   The gold fever broke out,
'N' I'd hev been a pioneer
   Without the slightest doubt,
But Molly, here, took on 'n' said,
   "Ar go naut, dearest Joe!"
I thought I'd argy not with her,
   So, boys, I didn't go.

134

WHAT'S HONOR.

Ask not the soldier in the battle's van,
  Nor yet the statesman, uncorrupt as gold,
But her beneath your own roof-tree, who can,
  And will most willingly, to you unfold
The secret. Bid her mark your neighbor's wife
  When she her ample wardrobe seeks, to don her
Fine garments; when she reappears, my life
  I'll stake, your better half can tell what's on her.

CASABIANCA.

The boy stewed on the burning deck,
    Whence all but him had fled;
And when they shouted, "Leave the wreck!"
    He turned and hotly said,
"I'm goin' down with this 'ere ship—¬
    Hulk, mast, jib-boom, and spanker;
And when I've made my briny trip,
    You'll find Casa-by-anchor."

135

SHARP SHOOTING.

" I'M an archer, dear, no longer,"
 Said a maiden fair and bright
To her beau, with lip a-quiver—
 " Webster says, 'Toxophilite.'"

Then she gave her beau a narrow,
 Searching glance, with pert grimace,
While he thought his love was archer
 Than Diana in the chase.

" William Tell me how you like it;"
 " Well enough," replied the wight;
" It is true, among the archers,
 Oftentimes, talk's awful light."

THE END.

THE STARTLING EXPLOITS OF DR. J. B. QUIÈS.

From the French of PAUL CÉLIÈRE. By Mrs. CASHEL HOEY and Mr. JOHN LILLIE. Profusely Illustrated. Crown 8vo, Extra Cloth, $1 75.

It is one of the best bits of fun we have read for a long time—we may even say the very best bit of that kind of fun which is pronounced without being too broad or too boisterous.—*The Spectator*, London.

This enchanting book should become one of the most popular among the season's novelties. The artist's work is worthy of Bertall in his prime.—*Saturday Review*, London.

The book abounds in laughable situations, arising from the conflict between the doctor's desire to be at rest and the perverse fate which urges him on, and it will be read with unflagging interest.—*Christian at Work*, N. Y.

The conception is carried out in a very novel manner; in his guileless simplicity and childishness the doctor is a fit companion to Mr. Pickwick, and he must be a chronic dyspeptic who does not find himself laughing over the healthful humor with which the book fairly bubbles over.—*Philadelphia Record*.

We commend Dr. Quiès to tired, bored, overworked, and, sadder yet, underworked readers, who will welcome so fresh and bright a writer as Célière with keen relish.—*Chicago Tribune*.

The learned doctor is subjected to a series of wonderful adventures, the contemplation of which, heightened by the wit and vivacious style of the author, cannot fail to cause the reader to indulge in constant laughter at his expense. . . . Nearly every page is handsomely illustrated. The engravings are artistic, and admirably reflect the spirit of the author.—*Albany Press*.

A piece of perfectly delicious French wit. The adventures are droll, and the circumstances are stated with a detail and fidelity that are surprisingly well sustained. The character of the doctor is cleverly drawn, and one cannot read his adventures without being broken up by the irresistible wit of the book.—*Hartford Daily Courant*.

PUBLISHED BY HARPER & BROTHERS, NEW YORK.

☞ *The above work sent by mail, postage prepaid, to any part of the United States or Canada, on receipt of the price.*

THE ADVENTURES OF JIMMY BROWN.

Written by himself, and Edited by W. L. ALDEN. Illustrated. 16mo, Extra Cloth, $1 00.

It recounts the offences of a lively boy against the proprieties and conventionalities of society, and is as full of excellent fun as it can well be. Unlike certain books of its class, which portray vulgarity if not vice, the boyish pranks here recorded will bring no blush of shame to the reader.—*Chicago Interior.*

This Jimmy Brown, who tells his stories in a boy's way, is an especially observing and critical little fellow, and he very naturally often makes surprises by his amount of knowledge and his unconscious estimates of character. It is an entertaining book for juveniles and older people.—*St. Louis Republican.*

This is one of the most amusing books for young people ever issued from the American press. It relates the ludicrous experiences of a bright and mischievous boy, who gets himself and other people into all sorts of trouble in making practical application of the instruction received from his parents and teachers.—*Albany Press.*

It is a most fascinating book, full of amusement for old and young, and wholly free from evil of every kind, which last is a thing, unfortunately, that cannot be truly said of many of the humorous books of the time intended for juvenile perusal.—*N. Y. Commercial Advertiser.*

It is a genuine boy's book, and so thoroughly reflects boy nature and boy mischief, and is so completely in harmony with boy thought and boy methods of reflection that it seems almost an emanation of one of the most restless and most unreflecting of that amusing tribe.—*Boston Gazette.*

These short sketches of scrapes into which Jimmy Brown, a mischievous boy, unhappily falls, are written in Mr. Alden's funniest vein. They will please the boys of all classes. There is fun enough in the book to keep the average boy laughing for several months. They are decidedly ingenious as well as humorous.—*Cincinnati Commercial-Gazette.*

Mr. Alden's wit . . . is always of a character that amuses without leaving any feeling of annoyance or dissatisfaction behind it.—*N. Y. Times.*

PUBLISHED BY HARPER & BROTHERS, NEW YORK.

☞ *The above work sent by mail, postage prepaid, to any part of the United States or Canada, on receipt of the price.*

COX'S WHY WE LAUGH.

Why We Laugh. By SAMUEL S. COX. 12mo, Cloth, $1 50; 4to, Paper, 25 cents.

The lovers and appreciators of good things throughout the length and breadth of the land will rise up and call him blessed for what he has here gathered together for their delectation. . . . Especially rich are his descriptions of passages at arms on the floor of Congress, in which such men as Randolph, Clay, Hale, Tristam Burgess, Tom Corwin, Ben Hardin, Proctor Knott, Douglas, Butler, Schenck, Nye, John Cochrane, and others took part. Here we get dozens of anecdotes which are thoroughly fresh.—*Boston Transcript.*

Mr. Cox has rare skill as a *raconteur,* and always clusters his anecdotes, jokes, retorts, epigrams, and quiddities in such a way that they emphasize and illustrate each other.—*Appleton's Journal,* N. Y.

It is a book to read, to laugh over, and to enjoy.—*Albany Journal,* N. Y.

Contains the largest, best, and most amusing collection of American "quips and jests," wit and humor, racy anecdotes, and ready retorts yet put together.—*Philadelphia Press.*

A chapter of this is a better remedy for indigestion than a bushel of invisible pills; and the book itself is an admirable prophylactic for most of the maladies of man.—*Commercial Bulletin,* Boston.

Mr. Cox's book, we are sure, will entertain the reader, whoever he may be, who takes it up to divert a dull hour.—*N. Y. Evening Post.*

It is a book of good humor, which keeps the muscles of the reader relaxed, and provokes a pleasant inward merriment which lubricates all the joints of the mind and sets all the kind feelings gently flowing. Mr. Cox has made a really good book, which will diffuse happiness wherever it circulates.—*N. Y. Daily Graphic.*

The volume is both amusing and instructive, and contains enough novelty of matter and treatment to give it a place in literature and recommend it to the reading, thinking, laughing world.—*St. Louis Republican.*

Mr. Cox makes out a very good case for American humor, and illustrates its different phases with spirit and intelligence.—*Chicago Inter-Ocean.*

PUBLISHED BY HARPER & BROTHERS, NEW YORK.

☞ *The above work sent by mail, postage prepaid, to any part of the United States or Canada, on receipt of the price.*

BONNER'S DIALECT TALES.

Dialect Tales. By Sherwood Bonner. 8vo, Cloth, $1 75.

These sketches are both entertaining and interesting. They are full of genial and healthy humor, and embody the results of a remarkably keen observation.—*The Critic, N. Y.*

All the stories deal with curious phases of life and character at the South, and afford a realistic and entertaining glimpse of persons and things not to be met with elsewhere; the delineations of negroes, their ways and ideas, and of moonshiners, and the wild conditions of existence among these outlaws being specially strong and telling. The stories are full of humorous situations and amusing dialogues, while the style is brilliant and racy.—*Boston Post.*

There could be nothing more inimitable of their kind, and absolutely perfect in their way, than these humorous and pathetic tales by Sherwood Bonner. The imitation of the negro dialect, of negro traits, characteristics, habits, manners, is absolutely faultless and true to the very life.—*New Orleans Times-Democrat.*

The individuals and scenes are realistic as photographs. . . . No such crisp, breezy, vigorous stories have appeared in any single volume since Bret Harte's earliest and best; with the flavor of wild fruit in them, and a spirited personality that would have to assert itself wherever it was.—*Literary World, Boston.*

As a representation of manners, this collection of stories has quite a positive value, while those who read for entertainment's sake alone ought to find abundant amusement in its several chapters.—*Philadelphia Telegraph.*

Sherwood Bonner's book is overflowing with quaint humor, and some of the incidents so delightfully told would cause the most confirmed dyspeptic to forget his ills. "Dialect Tales" is handsomely illustrated, and will furnish many an evening's pleasure about the fireside.—*Buffalo Express.*

They are studies from life by a close observer with a kindly touch, who feels sincerely the passion as well as the absurdity, the pathos as well as the fun, of her subject.—*Boston Transcript.*

One of the most entertaining books it has been our luck to read for a long time.—*N. Y. Herald.*

Published by HARPER & BROTHERS, New York.

☞ *The above work sent by mail, postage prepaid, to any part of the United States or Canada, on receipt of the price.*

www.ingramcontent.com/pod-product-compliance
Lightning Source LLC
Chambersburg PA
CBHW020407030726
47496CB00007B/2340

* 9 7 8 3 7 4 2 8 9 9 6 0 6 *